W9-AGD-365

This book belongs to:

Name: _ _ _ _ _ _ _ _ _ _ _ _ _ _ _ _

Favorite season: _ _ _ _ _ _ _ _ _ _

Planters & Cultivators
with Casey & Friends
It's spring on Happy Skies Farm. Time to work on this year's crops!
Tammi and Sammy are already in the fields. Let's go!
T

Creating the Right Team for Growing Crops

Casey's team is specially designed to work without harming the soil. That's because a successful harvest needs soft, healthy soil. In spring, the team cultivates the fields to prepare them for planting seeds. And in the fall, the team feeds and protects the fields for the next year. Keeping the soil healthy is a full-time job!

The Science of Soil

Kellie Gathers a Great Harvest

Tammi Prepares the Seeds' Bed

Peter Protects the Crops

Evan Plants Perfect Rows

Casey Feeds the Crops

The Science of Soil

Soil is made up of four parts: minerals (sand, silt, and clay), water, air, and organic matter (material from dead plants and animals). There are different types of soil, but each one is made up of these four parts. The differences depend on how much of each part is in the soil.

THE WORM CAVE!

5

Tammi Prepares the Seeds' Bed

Once the snow melts and the ground warms up, Sammy and I till the fields. I break up hard clumps of soil and make the fields even. Tilling in the spring prepares the soil for planting.

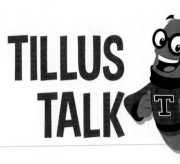

TILLUS TALK

Twice Is Nice!

Tammi tills the fields two times—in the spring and fall.

Fall tillage cuts up plant pieces so they can mix into the soil.

Spring tillage levels the fields so crops will grow evenly.

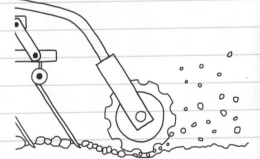

Side Note:

Certain fields don't get tilled as much because they need protection from heavy rain and wind. For example, loose-tilled soil on hillsides could wash down a hill in a rainstorm.

The Hard Truth About Compaction

The plant's roots naturally explore soil to find food and water. If the roots hit something hard, they grow around it. But what happens if all the soil is hard? The roots grow out rather than down—and that's not good. For this reason, farmers work hard to make their soil soft.

Look what happens to the plant when there is a hard compaction layer in the soil. Why do you think this would be a problem for Casey's crops?

Soft soil allows a plant's roots to grow down. Roots that reach far into the earth can soak up food and water, especially when the weather is hot and dry.

TILLUS TALK

Nature's Tiny Tillers

Over time, Mother Nature does a great job tilling the soil with her own equipment—worms like me!

We dig tunnels in the soil in search of food. The tunnels let air and water soak into the soil. Plus, we leave organic matter in the soil— our poop!

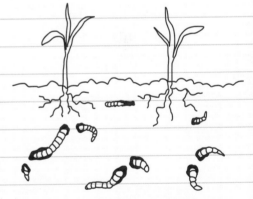

Make the Connection!

How are Tammi and Tillus alike?

9

The Big Picture in Planting Row Crops

Once the soil is prepared and is warm enough, I begin planting! It takes many steps to plant a seed into the soil, and my row units do all the work! Each unit has many parts that work so quickly it looks like all the steps happen at one time. As a result, I am able to plant hundreds of seeds in a minute!

1 Row Unit

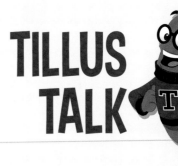
Planters Are Perfectionists!

Evan works quickly, but he never makes a mistake.

He plants every seed at exactly the same depth and space from one another.

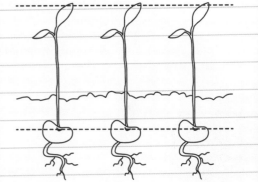

The spacing allows for equal amounts of sunlight to shine on every plant.

When the plants grow, they will all be the same height!

Make the Connection!

Why is corn called a row crop?

11

A Seed's Adventure

The healthiest crops begin with good seeds. But a seed's journey starts before it even reaches the ground. Let's follow a seed as it travels from tank to soil!

1

2

1. Casey pours seeds into big seed tanks at the top of the planter.

2. The seeds are blown through a series of hoses to individual row units.

3. A vacuum sucks the seeds into the Advanced Seed Meter.

4. Seeds travel around the seed meter disk— like riding on a Ferris wheel!

5. Three spools knock off any seed buddies trying to ride the disk with their friends. It's important that Evan plants only one seed at a time!

6. The single seed is dropped into the trench. Now it's ready to grow!

Evan's Row Units

Evan has 16 individual row units that plant seeds. Each unit works independently from the others. It's like having 16 separate planters working together at one time!

① ② ③ ④ ⑤ ⑥

① LEADING EDGE OFFSET OPENERS

Slices through residue and hard soil. It prepares soil for a clean trench.

② FURROW FORMING POINT

Forms a clean, V-shaped trench. Unlike a W-shaped trench, the V-shape guarantees that the seeds fall in the same point.

③ SEED PROTECTION SHOE

Prevents loose soil from falling into trench before the seed is dropped. The seed drops from the middle of the seed protection shoe.

④ PULLED GAUGE WHEEL

These wheels ride up and over obstacles like a wheelbarrow. The inside walls of the tires are soft to keep the soil mounded on the sides of the trench.

⑤ INVERTED OFFSET CLOSING DISKS

Replaces soil into the trench from both sides, so moist soil covers the seed. It "zips" the trench up from bottom to top.

⑥ ZERO-PRESSURE CLOSING WHEEL

Seals the soil on top of the trench. The wheel presses a special pattern into the soil that will help guide water to the planted seeds.

Case Study: Corn

The United States grows more corn than any other country in the world. That's because corn plants like the weather and soil found in states like Iowa, Illinois, Indiana, Minnesota, Nebraska, Ohio, and Kansas.

In the summer months, these states have sunny, warm days; cooler nights; and plenty of rain. Perfect for growing corn!

CORN BELT

Parts of a Corn Plant

------ height 8-14 ft.

tassel

silk

ear

leaf

stem

roots

Kernels are the seeds of a corn plant. They are arranged in paired rows on the ear of corn. If early growing conditions are good, the ear will have more rows. If growing conditions are good late in the season, the rows will be longer.

Milk Line

Black Layer

Pairs

Think It Through:

1. Why are Iowa, Illinois, Indiana, Kansas, Minnesota, Nebraska, and Ohio called the Corn Belt?

2. Why can't corn grow in Iowa during the winter?

3. Why do you think corn needs a lot of space to grow? (Hint: Look at the picture of a corn plant!)

Casey Feeds the Crops

Each year, I test the soil in my fields to see how healthy it is. If the soil lacks certain nutrients, I put them back in with fertilizer. I have the fertilizer specially made to contain the right amounts of minerals my soil needs. I am a soil scientist!

TILLUS TALK

The Scoop on Poop

Some farmers fertilize with manure (animal poop!).

Manure is made up of digested grasses and grains.

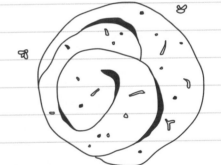

It contains nutrients, like nitrogen, which is good for plants.

Worms help to break down manure into organic matter—an important part of soil.

Go Tillus!

Side Note:

Nitrogen gives soil a "boost" of nutrients to help it grow crops.

19

Fertilizer, Floaters, and Tillage

Casey can fertilize the fields in the fall or spring. She uses a floater to spread nutrients on top of the soil. Then, I till the fields after the floater fertilizes. The floater and I work together to make sure the nutrients mix into the soil.

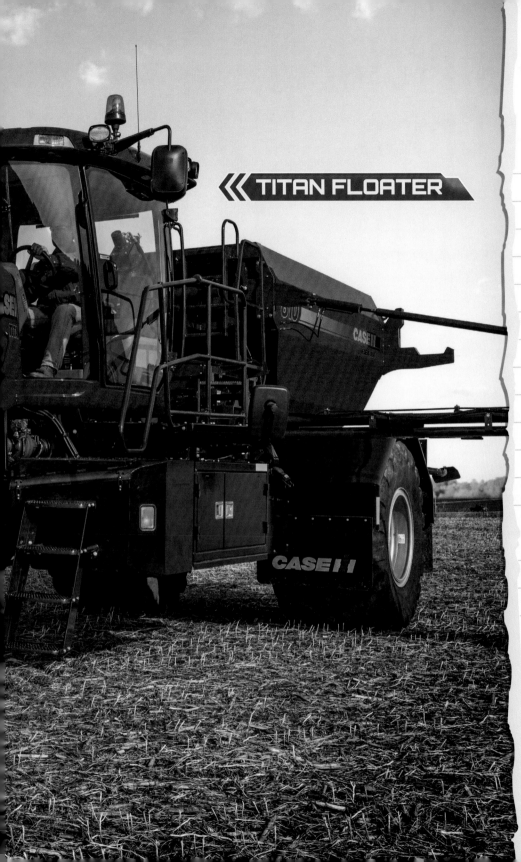

‹‹‹ TITAN FLOATER

TILLUS TALK

What's in a Name?

Floaters have extra large tires to help them "float" over the fields.

The 3-wheel floater is designed so that its tires don't follow one another over the fields.

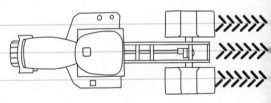

That reduces compaction and keeps the soil healthy, soft, and spongy!

Side Note:

Fertilizer comes in dry and liquid forms. And a floater can spread both forms!

Peter Protects the Crops

Danger buzzes in the air and lurks underground! So it's my job to protect the young crops from hungry insects and pushy weeds. My sprinklers spray a protective shield around each seedling.

TILLUS TALK

Peter's in Control!

Peter makes sure to give each plant the right amount of protection.

Casey can control the drop size and amount of liquid that sprays from each of his sprinkler nozzles.

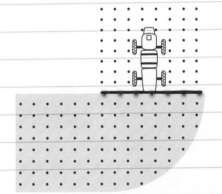

She can shut off sections of Peter's boom sprinklers, so he doesn't spray the same area twice.

Make the Connection!

Why do you think Casey sometimes needs to shut off parts of his boom? Hint: She does it when they turn corners.

23

Kellie Gathers a Great Harvest & Nourishes the Fields for Next Year's Crops

Tammi, Evan, and Peter have done a great job cultivating and planting the crops! As a result, this year's harvest is bigger than ever. But even as I gather this year's crops, I begin work on next season's planting.

TILLUS TALK

Breaking Down to Build Up

Kellie and Cody feed the soil for next year's crops.

They chop up leftover pieces of plant, called chaff or residue.

They spread the chaff on the fields.

The chaff nourishes the soil and protects it from winter storms.

Side Note:

Leftover pieces of plant feed worms. Yum!

Casey Maintains the Team

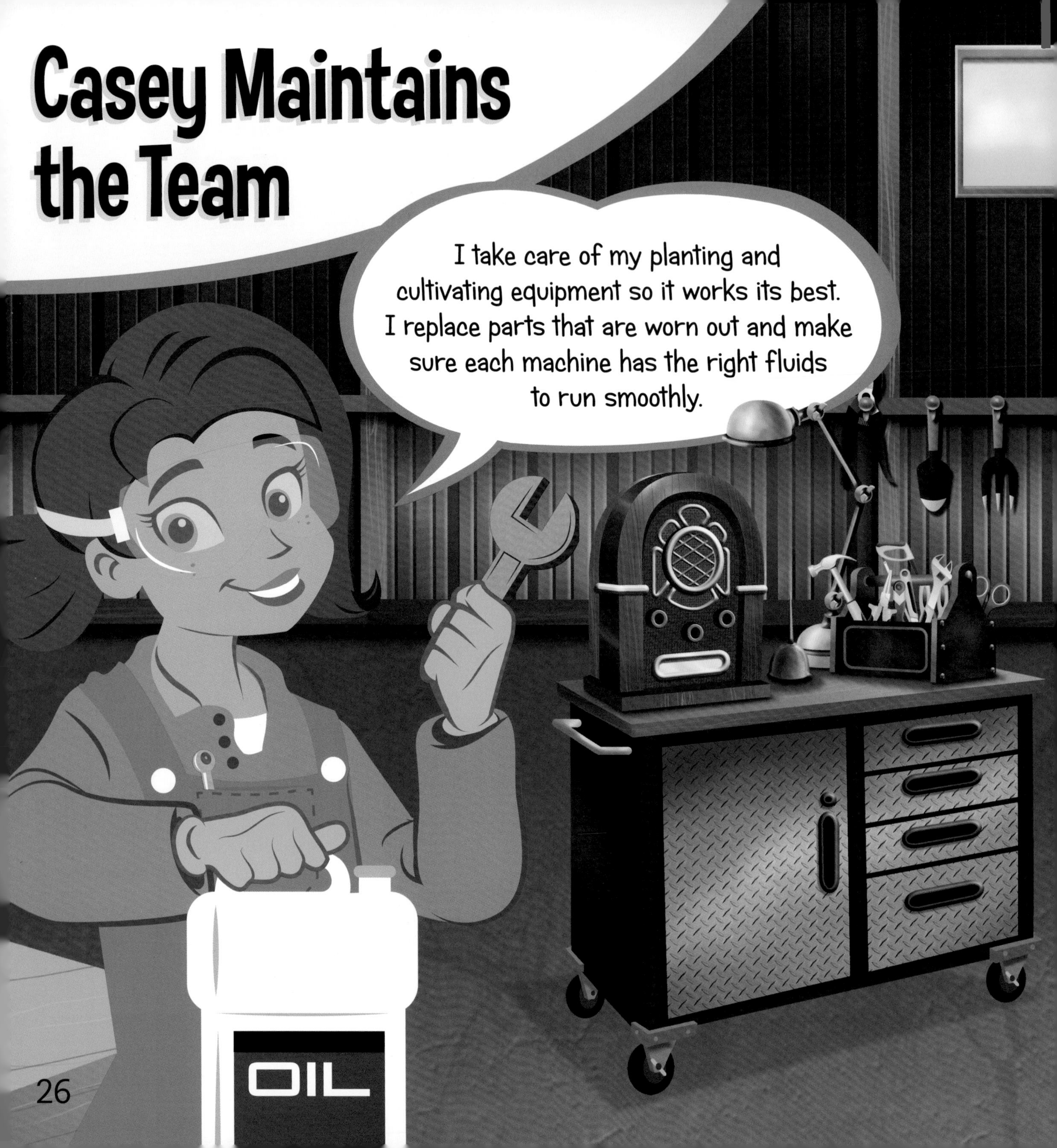

After we finish our work for the season, Casey makes sure we are in top shape for next year. Then, she washes us until we sparkle like new. Now we're ready for a well-deserved nap over the winter!

27

Experiment: Planting Seeds

This experiment will help you understand why Evan plants every seed at the same depth.

LESSON PLAN

MATERIALS
You will need:

- 3 clear plastic cups labeled #1, #2, #3
- potting soil
- 3 bean seeds
- water
- a ruler
- a sunny place to grow your seeds

PROCEDURE

1/2"

SEED

#1

Put 1" of soil at the bottom of cup #1. Place 1 bean seed on top of the soil. Fill the cup with soil, leaving a ½" space at the top.

1/2"

SEED

#2

Fill cup #2 halfway up with soil. Place 1 bean seed on top of the soil. Fill the cup with soil, leaving a ½" space at the top.

1/2"

SEED

#3

Fill cup #3 with soil leaving 1" of space at the top. Place 1 bean seed on top of the soil. Fill the cup with ½" of soil, leaving a ½" space at the top.

Water each cup with the same amount of liquid and place the cups in a sunny place. Water your plants when the soil feels dry.

Look at your cups once a day for two weeks. Write down what you see. Do you see a sprout? What does it look like? How big is it?
Did your seeds grow at the same time? How were they different? How were they the same? Can you think of a way to make them grow so they look exactly the same?

GLOSSARY

BOOM

the long section on a sprayer where the sprinklers are located

FERTILIZER

special material spread on soil to help grow plants

CHAFF OR RESIDUE

parts of the plant other than grain that are chopped into small pieces and spread on the field

COMPACTION

when a lot of weight presses down on soil and makes it packed tightly together

FLOATER

a large machine used to spread fertilizer on fields

CULTIVATE

preparing soil to make it healthy for growing plants

INDEPENDENTLY

thinking or acting for oneself

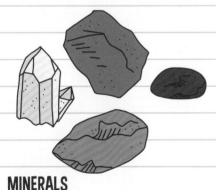

NOURISH

to feed or give healthful food

ROW UNIT

the part of a planter that plants one row of seeds

MANURE

animal poop that is used to fertilize the soil

NUTRIENTS

the nourishing part in food that living things need to grow and survive

ORGANIC MATTER

materials from dead plants and animals

MINERALS

broken down rocks that are naturally formed under the ground

TILLAGE

preparing soil for planting seeds

31

FUN FACTS!

Tilth is the physical condition of soil.
Happy crops need healthy tilth!

Fields prepared to plant crops in are called seedbeds.

INDIANA   IOWA   NEBRASKA

There are about 20,000 different
soil types in the United States.

Some farmers use aircraft to spray and protect their fields.

The tread of the closing wheel on a planter is designed
to look like a bird footprint.

There are about 6,000 different types of earthworms.

Hard red winter wheat is planted in fall and harvested in spring.

Some planters can plant up to 36 rows at one time.

Octane Press, Edition 1.0, March 1, 2016

© 2016 CNH Industrial America LLC. All rights reserved. Case IH, IH, and Farmall are trademarks registered
in the United States and many other countries, owned by or licensed to CNH Industrial N.V., its subsidiaries, or affiliates.

All rights reserved. With the exception of quoting brief passages for the purposes of review,
no part of this publication may be reproduced without prior written permission from the publisher.

Library of Congress Cataloging-in-Publication Data

ISBN-13: 978-1-937747-55-8 ISBN: 1937747558

1. Juvenile Nonfiction—Transportation—General. 2. Juvenile Nonfiction—Lifestyles—Farm and Ranch Life.

3. Juvenile Nonfiction—Lifestyles—Country Life. 4. Juvenile Nonfiction—Concepts—Seasons

Library of Congress Control Number: 2014954260

octanepress.com

Printed in the United States